The Dumpy Princess

*How a plain little girl with no chin
became Queen of England*

The Dumpy Princess

Karin Fernald

Illustrated by Sophie Foster

F

FRANCES LINCOLN
CHILDREN'S BOOKS

For Carys – *K.F.*
For my mum – *S.F.*

Chapter One

There was once a dumpy princess with no money, no friends and no chin. She had bulging blue eyes and a beaky nose; she was short and a bit plump. But her eyes were bright, her skin was clear and her hair was the colour of almonds. Her name was Princess Victoria.

Princess Victoria had four bad uncles. Uncle William had ten children and no wife. Uncle Frederick cheated at cards. Uncle Ernest had murdered several people, though nobody could prove it. Uncle George, who ate much too much, was fond of his bottle and unkind to his wife. He was King of England.

Then there was Uncle
Augustus, who was very odd,
and Uncle Adolphus, who was
gentle and liked sewing. His
friends called
him Dolly.

These six uncles were brothers
and they all hated each other, except
Uncle Adolphus. There was one more
brother: Edward, Duke of Kent,
Victoria's father. The
other brothers hated
him and he loathed them back.

Edward, Duke of Kent was
a soldier, not wicked, but fierce.
He was tall and stout, with thick,
black, bushy eyebrows, and he had
bulgy, blue eyes like Victoria's, but
not as pretty. He was bald, and so
is Victoria when this story begins,
with just a few tufts of shiny hair –
because she had been born only five
months before.

One dull morning in early November, she was lying in her frilly white cot, when in marched her father all glittering. His broad chest was covered with silver medals, and his high, black boots were polished like diamonds.

"Victoria," said Edward, Duke of Kent, sitting carefully down in his tight army trousers. "I want to tell you a story. It's important. It's to do with you." The medals clinked prettily.

His daughter smiled. "U-u-u-rr-hh-h," said Victoria warmly.

"Attention!" bellowed the Duke. "Far away, beyond this palace, and beyond the palace gardens,  and beyond a lot of other places, too, Victoria, that you won't have got to grips with yet, there lies a Great Rock. It is called the Rock of Gibraltar. There the sun shines hot all day, and the sky is blue and the monkeys play."

"O-o-ooo-hh-h!" said Victoria, wiggling her toes.

"Yes," agreed her father. "It's a fine place. Now, listen." (The Duke enjoyed the sound of his own loud voice.) "There I was one morning, up on this Great Rock, eating a strawberry ice, punishing soldiers, can't remember why. Five hundred lashes each, did 'em good. Up comes this dirty old foreign woman with her hand stretched out. 'Get away, hag,' said I. 'Jump off the cliff.' And what do you think she said?"

The Duke peered enquiringly down at his baby daughter, eyes bulging.

"U-u-u-uuuuurrrrhhh," said Victoria vaguely, examining her fingers and thumbs.

Her father raised his voice. "What the old witch said was this," he boomed. "'Listen to me', she croaked, 'Edward, Duke of Kent,' — that's me, you know, Victoria — 'you don't deserve it, but good fortune is coming your way. Stop beating those poor soldiers. They've done nothing worse than usual. Cross my palm with silver, and I'll tell you your good fortune.'"

The Duke leaned forward over the rail of the frilly white cot. "And then," he said, "the old crone did just that. Are you following me so far, Victoria?"

His daughter pointed a wandering, fat finger at her father's dyed black moustache.

"Goo!" she said.

"What she told me was," persisted the Duke, "that one day I, Edward, Duke of Kent, would have a little daughter who would grow up to be a Great Queen and order people about. Of course," he sighed, "I'd have made a Great King myself, if it weren't for those brothers of mine, curse them. Now," said the Duke, leaning still further forward, clutching the rail of the cot, "I haven't any other little daughters, none to speak of, that is. Only you, Victoria. So the Great Queen must be you. You must be Her."

"A-a-aarrhhh," said Victoria, starting to dribble. The Duke hated wet babies. He got up as quickly as he could in his tight trousers, medals jangling, and prepared to leave the room.

"So eat your carrots and greens," he ordered, "and grow up strong and commanding and tall, like me. Then you'll be able to tell other people what to do. You'll enjoy that. None of those uncles will want you to be Queen. Especially Uncle George, or Uncle Ernest, for that matter. Take no notice."

"Da," said Victoria to herself. The Duke thought she was trying to say "Daddy", and left the room happy. Soon afterwards, he went for a walk on a cold rainy day, got his feet wet, forgot to dry them, caught a bad cold and died.

Victoria's mother wept and wept, wearing black from head to foot. She was German, so she wept in German. "Alas, my dear darlink Edvard," she cried, over her daughter's cot, "If you hat only triet your trouzers ant socks! How can I liff vidout you?"

"U-u-uuUUUUURGH!" complained Victoria, lonely in her cot. Its frills were black now, and she was in black too, like a large, lacy beetle.

Her mother picked her up and hugged her.

"How can I liff all alone," the Duchess wailed, "in dis treadful strange country, vidout my dear Edvard who looked after me so vell? You too, Vicky!" The Duchess buried her wet face in her daughter's frills.

"Before you vere born, vile you vere still inside me, he trove us bose hundrets of miles from my homelant, just so dat you could be born here in Enklant, ent haf a good chance of being de Qveen!"

"AAAARGGGHHH!!!" objected Victoria, black frills soggy from her mother's tears.

The Duchess lifted her face, still holding her daughter close.

"Vat a lonk journey it vos!" she recalled. "But he trove de coach and de horses zo smoozly, I vas neffer in de least bit sick! Not vunce!"

"Da!" said Victoria, drier now, and glad of a cuddle. "DA! DA!"

"Ah!" cried her mother. "De dear chilt remembers her fader! How fine he vos! And vot a great kink he vould haf mate, eef his horrid brudders hadn't been born before him. How dey all hated each udder! Dey'll hate me too, I know, and my poor little chilt!"

"DaDA!" said Victoria. The Duchess cheered up for a moment, but soon began weeping again, louder than before.

Chapter Two

Victoria's mother had dark eyes and dark hair. She wore big hats with feathers on, and shiny, rustly silk dresses, and looked very pretty most of the time. She loved painted china scent-bottles and elegant, silver-framed mirrors and brightly enamelled pin-boxes that the Duke had given her with the last of their money. She loved painting and drawing too, and she wrote cheerful tunes in her spare time.

They lived in a red-brick palace in London. It stood in a fine park with lakes, swirling willows, little trees cut with big scissors into shapes like balloons and grand sweeps of lawn. The palace itself, though, was huge and cold. Its ground floor, where Victoria and her mother lived, was gloomy and dark, with no view over the beautiful park. And bits of it were always falling down because the Duchess of Kent didn't have the money to keep it standing up.

In fact, Victoria's mother didn't have money for anything much. Often she couldn't pay the butcher, the greengrocer or the baker, which upset her a lot, though not as much as it upset them.

"Von't you let me haf a few pennies?" she asked one afternoon in her best English, her best feathered hat, her best blue-and-lilac silk dress and her most charming smile. She was speaking to Victoria's Uncle George, King of England, the only person she knew who had any pennies at all. "I vos your dear brudder's vife, after all, and my little daughter, your niece, may vell be Qveen vun day."

They were in the grand drawing-room of St James's Palace. The Duchess stood respectfully, toes pinched in her best shoes. Uncle George sprawled all over a large couch. Beside it stood a polished table with cakes and tea-things for one, and bottles filled with strong-smelling drinks.

"You must be joking," said Uncle George, pouring himself a large brandy. "I had to wait twenty years to be King. Now my stupid old father's kicked the bucket at last, I'm jolly well going to be King for ever! So would you, if you were me!"

"Dat's right," said the Duchess politely, hoping for a cup of tea.

"And why does everyone think I'm made of money?" said wicked Uncle George, tucking into a cream doughnut. "Well, I am, actually, and I'm going to keep it to myself."

"Naturally," said the Duchess, wishing he would

offer her a chair. She tried easing the toes of one foot inside its tight shoe, and smiled brightly at Uncle George.

"Take my advice," he said, a splodge of cream running down his chin, "Go back to where you came from. You'll never manage in this country. Your English is no good, and never will be. You haven't got the ear."

He wiped his chin with an embroidered silk napkin. "Here's sixpence towards your boat fare," he said finally, as he finished the doughnut and began on a chocolate-covered banana ice stuffed with raisins and nuts.

The Duchess left, toes cramped, head held high. She didn't take the sixpence or the advice. She would have liked to go home to Germany, where people liked her and understood what she said. But she knew that the Duke wanted her to stay in England with Victoria. And that's what she was going to do, come what may.

Chapter Three

By the time she was three years old, it was clear to all the servants in the palace that Princess Victoria had a bad temper. "AARRGH!!" she would scream at the nurse who tried to wash her, and the maid who tried to dress her, and the tutor who tried to teach her the ABC. She would boil inside, stamp her feet one after the other and yell the palace down in a loud voice like her father's, only higher.

Still more, she hated having to sit still while the Duchess listened to strange people talking on and on – such as old men from the Church of England (bishops, they were called) who used to come and sit about for hours, and wanted to see Victoria.

Those old men look very odd, she thought. *Why do they wear long dresses like Mamma?*

And why are their fronts covered with aprons? Victoria wore an apron herself at meals, but not all the time. *They must be very messy,* she thought, *even though they've had more practice than me at not spilling things.*

Even odder was their hair: curly, greyish-white and very long. Most men Victoria saw in the palace had short hair, and so did she. She couldn't understand these long, grey curls. She wanted to get to the bottom of them. One day, the Bishop of Chichester came to lunch. He wore a long dress and apron, and his hair was particularly curly and greyish-white. Victoria sat next to him on her high chair. The Bishop talked on and on, his head turned away. Victoria stretched out a hand, took a bunch of his curls, gently, and shook them, just to see what would happen.

All of a sudden, the air was filled with thick dust! It nearly blinded her, and made her sneeze.

"*Utchoo!*" said Victoria, grabbing the curls harder.

The Bishop laughed, and moved his head about a little, but not as if it hurt him. It was almost as if he couldn't feel his own hair, not at all…

And then, his WHOLE HEAD slipped round a bit.

Victoria realized something disgusting: he couldn't

feel his hair because it wasn't his! The Bishop of Chichester was wearing FALSE HAIR!

"ARRGH!" screamed Victoria. Everyone choked and sneezed, including the Bishop, who kept laughing, and the Duchess of Kent, who didn't...

Victoria was removed from the table with no lunch. From then on, she never liked bishops, and yelled the palace down whenever she saw one.

Chapter Four

Vicky needs more names, thought the Duchess of Kent one day. *She iss, affter all, vun day perhaps Qveen...*

"Vot are der Qveens' names?" she asked aloud. The Duchess was seated at her dressing-table early one morning, while Janet the maid dressed her dark hair in high waves and coils.

"Queen Elizabeth, Madam." suggested Janet. "The most famous Queen ever."

"Zat's vot you English all say," said the Duchess. "And vhy not?" She had always enjoyed reading history. But, what with looking after Victoria and trying to keep the palace standing up, she didn't get much time for reading... Now her quick mind was starting to work.

"Aha!" she said. "Den perhaps der is also de name Georgina, affter her Uncle King George de Fourth! Dis vill perhaps varm dat selfish old heart!"

Later that day, the Duchess dressed herself

beautifully in plum silk, hair piled elaborately on top of her head, and spoke nicely to Uncle George.

"Vill you like dat?" she enquired, trying hard with her English and offering him a small whisky. It was tea-time at Kensington Palace.

"No," he said. "Too much ice. Up to the brim, woman. And for God's sake, do something about your English. It's frightful."

"Vot I meant voz," explained the Duchess, filling the glass with whisky up to the brim, "zese names I vant to gif my little dotter –

here iss a list. Haff a smoked salmon sandvich."

"Don't mind if I do," said Uncle George, taking three. "Now, let's see this list. Good God! Certainly not! I'm not having that child called after me! More whisky."

He poured a second glassful down his throat. "And can't you stop this silly jabbering?" he said to the Duchess rudely. "English is easy, never had a problem with it. One more for the road, if you don't mind. Down the hatch." Then he said, "Just call the wretched child Victoria, after Victory, and leave it at that."

And he polished off the last sandwich, took a final gulp of whisky, hitched up his robes and lurched off to carry on being King of England.

So the Duchess called her daughter Victoria, after Victory. She left it at that. And she decided that there was no point in being charming to Uncle George.

Chapter Five

Victoria had a half-sister called Feodora, twelve years older and beautiful, with dark eyes and hair. She was good at dancing, painting and drawing. She moved gracefully, had elegant, ladylike manners, and was admired by everybody, even Uncle George.

"I wish I was like you," said Victoria. They were in the palace gardens one afternoon in June. Feodora

was drawing the lake and the waterlilies and the ducks and the palace beyond. Victoria sat beside her trying to draw an imaginary dog with long ears. Or perhaps it was a rabbit? Victoria wasn't sure. A dog was what she had meant, but the legs were wrong.

"Try making them more knobbly," suggested Feodora. Victoria tried. The legs got worse.

Victoria had just begun dancing lessons. These were fun. That same morning, however, her dancing mistress, who was French, had said something odd.

"Princesse Victoria, you 'ave ze *corps ingrate*, ze ungrateful bodee!"

Victoria had been hurt. She knew that, as well as being dumpy, she was short for her age. But, even so, she had gone on trying to move gracefully all morning.

If you really want to be like me," said Feodora, pencilling in feathers on a duck, "you might try sitting up very straight. Or," she warned, "they'll do to you what they did to me. They pinned a huge bunch of holly on to my chest, to make me remember. I had to wear it all day long, for ages."

"How frightful!" exclaimed Victoria, and sat up very straight indeed in front of her long-haired dog (or rabbit).

Feodora finished her picture of the lake, and wrote *Feodora* at the bottom of it in clever squiggles and loops.

"...And another thing, Vicky," she said, "you talk with your mouth full."

"I don't!" protested Victoria.

"You do it all the time!" said her sister. "It's disgusting. Princesses aren't supposed to be disgusting. Especially if one day they may have to be Quee..."

"Be what?" asked Victoria.

"Er... Quack!" said Feodora. "See that duck? On its own, by the reeds? I was saying hallo to it. Over there!" Their mother didn't want Victoria to know that she might be Queen one day. It might over-excite her and make her ill – and when children got ill in those days, they often got worse and died.

Feodora changed the subject again.

"Why do you eat so much salt, Vicky?" she said sharply. "I've watched you at dinner. You mix masses of it in with your gravy. It looks greedy, and besides, salt's bad for you. It might be stopping you growing – I wouldn't be at all surprised if it were."

Victoria got up, scrunched her drawing and threw it as far as she could into the middle of the lake. Then she marched straight back into the palace without a word to her sister, nose in the air. Dinner would be plain and boring as usual. There was no cinnamon or cloves or coriander in those days, not in English kitchens anyway. Victoria wasn't going to put up with having no salt either. Besides, sometimes you had to put your foot down – both feet, in fact – or people would walk all over you and jump about – yes, even the nicest people.

Chapter Six

When Princess Feodora was twenty-one, she was married to a good-looking prince from Germany called Ernest, whom she liked very much. There was a grand wedding at St James's Palace. Victoria was a bridesmaid in a white lace dress with orange blossom in her hair. Her hair had to be done in ringlets: tight rags the night before, uncomfortable to sleep in, then burning-hot curling irons early the next morning. But it was worth it, for the party that evening.

There was a huge, marvellous white wedding cake shaped like a castle in the middle of a lake, with turrets and battlements and ramparts. On the lake swam a family of swans, made out of icing by Uncle George's French cook. Their feathers were so finely cut that they looked soft and real, and their orange beaks were marzipan.

Then there was syllabub, which Uncle George's French cook was specially good at and liked doing.

This was made of cream and ice-cream and oranges and sugar and lots of rose-petals so that it smelt of roses. Victoria ate three helpings. So did Uncle George, whom the Duchess had invited for the sake of his cook, and so that he would have to give Feodora a wedding present. The Duchess didn't speak a word to him, nor he to her.

Victoria went round all the guests, offering them each a flower from a wicker basket and having her ringlets admired. There was music and dancing, and ladies in glorious, rustling silk dresses and ribbons and bows, with tortoiseshell combs and coloured feathers in their curly, bouncy hair.

But when it was over, Feodora had to leave home for ever and go away with her prince to live in his great castle, which was very cold, he warned her. He was a poor prince, having lost all his money in wars which he hadn't started, so he couldn't afford to heat his castle properly. Worse still, this cold castle was in a distant part of Germany hundreds of miles away.

People travelled very slowly in those days, in cold, stuffy coaches along the roads, then by freezing ferry boat over the sea – and they were sick in the coaches and sick on the ferries. It might be years before the sisters met again, and they cried dreadfully at being parted.

They wrote to each other, and sent each other drawings. Feodora drew her castle, and the servants in the castle, and her prince, of course, and her babies, when she began having babies. And she drew the forest the castle stood in, and the animals in the forest. Victoria sent back drawings of her dogs. By now, she was getting rather good at them.

Chapter Seven

Victoria loved animals. She loved her parrot and her canary and her cat and her donkey and her little grey horse, Rosa. And she loved her dogs.

Her favourite dog was a black-and-white spaniel with long ears, whom she called Dash, because he was always dashing about. Dash loved Victoria in return. Sometimes, when he was tired from dashing about, he would stay still long enough for her to dress him up in a little red jacket and blue trousers, or to bath him, which she did every single day. She talked to him, too, all the time, when there was nobody else there.

From time to time, when he had something really important to say, Dash talked back.

Chapter Eight

Victoria had a governess called Lehzen to teach her history, geography, arithmetic and other things she needed to know. Lehzen was tall and thin, with beautiful dark eyes. The rest of her was nothing special to look at, but she dressed well and did her hair nicely. Lehzen was German, but she had learnt good English, and that's what she spoke to Victoria, who loved her.

Lehzen would sit still for hours while Victoria drew her from the front and the back and the side. She wanted to help Victoria to be good at doing whatever she had to do, so she showed her how to draw and to dress her dolls.

Victoria had over a hundred dolls. She and Lehzen named them after the singers and dancers they saw at the theatre. Victoria's favourite doll was named after a young dancer called Marie Taglioni, who could stand on tiptoe while dancing as if she was flying. Victoria admired her more than anyone, and loved the wooden doll named after her.

Victoria and Lehzen went out riding together every day. Victoria liked riding, even on a horse that jumped and kicked. Sitting on horseback made her feel taller. She was still very short for her age, which by now was ten years and a bit.

"Why worry about it?" said Lehzen, after one of their morning rides. They were in Victoria's sitting-room at a quarter to one. Lunch was late. "Tall people's blood doesn't reach their brains. It's got too far to go. They forget things. Lots of famous people have been short. Boney was short."

"Boney!" exclaimed Victoria, shivering down her back. "Oooh! Did you ever see him?"

"No, thank God," answered Lehzen, who was sewing lilac ribbons on to a new skirt for Marie Taglioni, "but I knew an old man who nearly saw him – his soldiers, at any rate."

"Ooo-er," gasped Victoria, She had heard about the terrible Boney – better known as Napoleon, the greatest soldier in the world, who frightened everybody – and about his wicked soldiers, whose burning and killing and stealing all over Europe had only been put a stop to just before she was born. "Tell me." And Victoria sat down on the carpet.

"When I was little," Lehzen said, "I was nosey. I wanted to know what was going on everywhere. I was the youngest of eight brothers and sisters."

"What fun you must have had!" said Victoria.

"My sisters didn't think so." answered Lehzen, looping one ribbon into a tiny lilac bow. "They had to try and find me! Once I ran away to our church and hid behind the boiler. From there I could see a little door, with steps leading up, very dark. I went up and up and up. And there was this old man with a long shiny tube! He poked it out of the window – hole in the wall, rather – and let me look down it from one end. And I could see over the fields and hills, very clearly. It was a telescope, of course. He spent all day, every day, looking out through it for Boney's soldiers!"

"And did he see them?" asked Victoria, half hoping so.

"No, thank God." answered Lehzen. She finished sewing her lilac bow and snipped off the thread. "If he had, they'd have been marching on our village, wouldn't they, and I wouldn't be here today!"

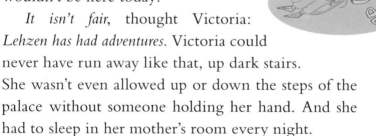

It isn't fair, thought Victoria: *Lehzen has had adventures.* Victoria could never have run away like that, up dark stairs. She wasn't even allowed up or down the steps of the palace without someone holding her hand. And she had to sleep in her mother's room every night.

"Please may I have my own room, Mamma?" she asked after lunch. "I need to be on my own sometimes, just for a bit."

"No, Vicky," said the Duchess firmly, and grew angry when Victoria asked why.

Lehzen must have had more fun, too, thought Victoria, *with eight brothers and sisters.*

"Can't we invite some of the children in Kensington Gardens into the Palace and have a party?" she asked at supper. "We could have fancy dress, and Punch and Judy, and dancing."

"No, Vicky," said her mother sharply, and Victoria went to bed feeling cross.

The Duchess had a good reason for keeping Victoria on her own. It was to do with one of her uncles, Ernest, Duke of Cumberland, who liked to terrify everybody. He was said to have tortured and killed several people, including one of his own servants, in order to steal the man's wife. The people of England dreaded him as much as they had dreaded Boney, if not more. And if it weren't for Princess Victoria, then one day Uncle Ernest would be King of England, because he was next in line to the Throne after her. And he wanted to be King very much indeed.

Any moment, thought the Duchess, *vicked Uncle*

Ernest or a vicked friend of his may slip into de Palace and stifle my little Vicky wid a fat pillow! Or push her down de stairs!

So, whenever Victoria went up or downstairs, someone had to hold her hand. She slept every night in her mother's room, and Lehzen stayed with her until the Duchess came to bed. Victoria never felt free for a moment, because her mother was so afraid of Uncle Ernest.

Chapter Nine

One morning after breakfast, Victoria went into her little bare schoolroom in Kensington Palace. She sat down at her desk as usual and opened her history book. Inside lay a sheet of paper that hadn't been there before.

She picked it up and looked at it, admiring its beautiful handwriting. It looked like Lehzen's writing, only it was especially neat. It was a list of all the kings and queens of England, from William the Conqueror, centuries back, right down to Victoria's own grandfather, King George III, who had not been quite right in the head. Then came Uncle George the Fourth, who was King still, but only just. Underneath Uncle George it said:

Next on Throne
Uncle William and Aunt Adelaide

Aunt Adelaide was Uncle William's new wife.

She was kind and sweet. They had had two little girl babies who had both died.

Poor Aunt Adelaide, thought Victoria. *I like her and she likes me. I expect she'll ask me to Buckingham Palace a lot, for tea.* As a rule, Victoria didn't get anything to eat between lunch and supper, so tea often crossed her mind.

I expect we'll have chocolate sponge and iced biscuits, and strawberry jelly and cream, she thought. Yes, the idea of kind Aunt Adelaide living at Buckingham Palace was very pleasant.

But Victoria hadn't finished reading this new sheet of paper. There was more writing at the bottom. She peered closely, and read:

Next on the Throne after them
Princess Victoria
(unless Aunt Adelaide has more babies)

Victoria stared, then blinked, then looked out of the window. She couldn't have read that last bit. She must have made it up. She looked back again at the sheet of paper.

Next on the Throne after them
Princess Victoria
(unless Aunt Adelaide has more babies)

Victoria went on staring at the sheet of paper, waiting for the words to change round and mean something else. But they stayed put, saying:

Next on the Throne after them
Princess Victoria
(unless Aunt Adelaide has more babies)

Victoria began to feel very heavy just above her stomach in between her ribs at the front, as if someone had hit her. She sat down in her upright school chair and tried breathing hard and deep, to make the feeling go away. But it wouldn't. She looked straight ahead.

She could see her life stretching ahead of her, with nobody to play with, ever – all dressed up, and buttoned and uncomfortable, having to sit down for ever and ever on a hard, golden throne with Bishops all round. The ache between her ribs grew worse.

They might have asked me, she thought. *Someone might have said 'Victoria, would you like to be Queen?' Why does it have to be me? Why can't someone else do it? Why can't someone else go and be Queen?*

And she began to cry, and went on crying, and cried until she gave herself a headache. Lehzen, who had been there all the time, brought her a little soft cloth dipped in cold water, and bound it round Victoria's aching head. Then she rang the bell, and asked Janet to bring some warm milk and sweet biscuits. Victoria drank the milk and ate the biscuits, and after a while she began to feel better. She found herself thinking: *Someone's got to be King or Queen. There's no other way. You don't want another Boney coming along. And it had better be someone who will do a good job. Not like Uncle George. Or Uncle Ernest. And not like my poor old grandfather King George the Third, who Mamma says was not quite right in the head. Maybe I'd better make the best of it. It's time there was a decent Queen. Perhaps, if I really try, I can be Her.*

So she dried her eyes, even though she hadn't stopped crying yet, and then hugged Lehzen for about five minutes. Lehzen hugged her back and said she thought that some of being Queen would be fun.

Then Lehzen went and woke up Dash, who was sleeping outside the door.

"How would you like to be a Queen's dog, Dash?" asked Victoria, still sitting in her upright schoolroom chair. "You'll be bathed every evening by a real Queen!"

"Good idea!" barked Dash, leaping round her. "Those biscuits look good. Perhaps a real queen won't get so much soap in my eyes!"

Well, then, thought Victoria, *perhaps my little grey*

horse Rosa would enjoy being fed sugar lumps by a future queen. The dolls would be pleased, too, because dolls are snobs, especially the beautiful, delicate Marie Taglioni, who was born to be a queen's doll, and knew it.

"But remember," said Lehzen thoughtfully, "perhaps your Aunt Adelaide will have more babies."

Chapter Ten

Soon King George the Fourth died, and Uncle William became King. Uncle William was sixty-five, and not well. He was excited about being King and had good ideas.

"Let's open Green Park to the public on Sunday afternoons," he said; and the public went and lay in Green Park with handkerchiefs over their heads, listened to the band playing, and ate sandwiches and drank beer. They liked Uncle William and hoped he would go on being King for a while, even though he was sixty-five and not well.

The public liked Aunt Adelaide too. She was much younger than Uncle William, and good and kind. She missed her two little princesses who had died, and it didn't look as if she was going to have any more. So she and Uncle William wanted to be friends with Victoria; and Victoria would have liked that too.

But there was one person who didn't want Victoria to be friends with anybody, especially with Uncle William and Aunt Adelaide. His name was Sir John Conroy.

Sir John Conroy was nearly as bad as Uncle Ernest. But while Uncle Ernest had a great many soldiers who did what he told them, Sir John Conroy only had one. This person did whatever he wanted, always, and she couldn't have been more important in the life of Princess Victoria: it was her mother, the Duchess of Kent.

The Duchess was lonely. She couldn't understand English jokes. She hadn't made friends with King George and she didn't feel like trying to make friends with King William.

Dese kinks! she thought miserably every morning, as she woke up. *Dey loathed my tear Edvard and dey loathe me! Dey vish to press me down! But no! I so vish to see again my home! My tear mudder, my sisters ant der little new babies! But I must remain for effer here in dis treadful Englant, for de sake off my Vicky!*

Sir John cheered her up, and she could understand his jokes. Besides, she remembered fondly, he had been friends with the Duke of Kent, Victoria's father. So the Duchess trusted Sir John completely.

This was a mistake.

Chapter Eleven

Sir John Conroy lived in Kensington Palace with his family, and pretended to look after the Duchess and Victoria. He was a tall, dark-haired man with a nicely-shaped nose and long legs.

"Let's be honest," he said to himself in his large bedroom mirror, one cold afternoon in early spring, "I'm a looker." He admired his nose in the mirror, sucked in his stomach and stuck out his chin.

"Film star, if you ask me," agreed his reflection in the mirror. "Only films haven't been invented yet."

"That's right," groaned Sir John. "Isn't life a mess? I'm wasted in this freezing old Palace, trying to play the clown. I ought to be a duke or something."

"Or Prime Minister?" suggested his reflection. "Looks count in a Prime Minister. Looks are the main thing."

Sir John shivered. He sat down on the bed, wrapping himself in a blanket. All this looking in the mirror made him feel worse. He forgot to suck in his stomach and buried his head in his hands. "Here I am," he muttered, "trailing after a silly foreign woman and her dreary little daughter. And I can't stand that child," he complained. "Face like a boiled egg."

He began to tear up letters from a great pile which lay on the bed. They were angry letters from people to whom he owed money.

"What've I got, after a lifetime of work at this and that?" he said. "A tiny bedroom in a freezing old palace that's falling to bits."

(Sir John had a bigger bedroom which he was supposed to share with his wife, Lady Conroy. But its mirror was small. So he usually came here instead, to this little bedroom with its big mirror, where he could admire himself properly.)

"Once she's Queen," he said, "that child's going to have money coming out of her ears. She won't know how to spend it. That child doesn't need money. She needs an egg-cup."

He carefully folded an elaborate paper dart out of one of the angry letters on the bed. This cheered him up a bit.

"Well," said Sir John, gazing again at his reflection, "Let's look on the bright side."

"That's right," said his helpful reflection, wrapped in the blanket. "Remember, the Duchess does what you say. And that stupid little girl does whatever her mother tells her to, naturally. So once she's Queen, you can be Special Adviser to them both, and highly paid!"

Sir John aimed the paper dart out of the window, threw off the blanket and leapt up off the bed.

"Then perhaps I can have that big estate in Wales!" he said, brightening. "And the other one in the South of France. It's time I had some fun." He strode about the little cold room. "God knows, I deserve it."

He caught sight of himself in the mirror, smiling, and this time it cheered him up. He sucked in his stomach again, and stuck out his chin further.

"There aren't many men with looks like mine. And I'm witty, too!" he cried.

Then his eyes narrowed. His reflection frowned back.

"There's just one thing. Eggface mustn't get any ideas. Or she might want someone else to advise her. I mustn't let her think her own thoughts," he said, sitting down again on the bed to worry properly. "I can't have her believing she'll be any use as Queen without her mother and me. That's important." He squeezed his eyes shut to concentrate.

There's one thing I might try, he thought. *Why don't I start making the wretched child believe she's really ugly?*

Chapter Twelve

Next morning, when they got down from the table after breakfast, Sir John Conroy said to Victoria, "Turn round. I want to see you from the side."

"What for?" asked Victoria.

"Do as I say," said Sir John.

Victoria turned round.

"Now, who is it you remind me of?" said Sir John. "I know!" he exclaimed, with an annoying laugh. "It's your uncle, King George the Fourth! Of course! He didn't have any chin, and neither do you! Same bulgy eyes you've got, too. Rotten luck for a girl. I feel sorry for you."

Sir John had been horrid before, but not as openly. Victoria was amazed. She couldn't think how to answer him, so she said nothing.

"Your Uncle George wasn't much of a king, you know. Too fond of his bottle by half. Not your fault, I suppose," said Sir John in a kindly voice. "Still, it's amazing how much you look like him.

Could be twins. Or am I thinking of Silly Billy?"

Silly Billy was what the public called another of Victoria's uncles, the Duke of Gloucester.

"You could almost be him in a skirt," said Sir John merrily, crunching toast. "You're shorter than him, of course – oh, sorry, Princess, have I said something to upset you?"

That night after dinner, Victoria lay in bed, very still. Lehzen sat beside her on the bed as usual, waiting for the Duchess to come upstairs. She was sewing another dress for Marie Taglioni.

Victoria was unusually quiet.

"Is something the matter, Vicky?" said Lehzen gently. "Have you a stomach ache?"

"Lehzen," asked Victoria suddenly, "am I stupid?"

"Certainly not, Vicky," said Lehzen, "except when you make a fuss about nothing, and shout and cry. In some ways you are most intelligent, I think, and are becoming more so. You are beginning to work things out for yourself. Who has been saying you are stupid?"

"Sir John," answered Victoria.

"Take no notice, Vicky," said Lehzen. "What else has he been saying?"

"Nothing," said Victoria, sniffing, "except –"

"Except what?" asked Lehzen, gently.

"Except he keeps asking me when I'm going to grow! Queens are supposed to be commanding and tall. Oh, Lehzen..." – and she started to cry – "I'm almost thirteen, and I haven't grown for over a year! Perhaps nobody will ever notice I'm there! Perhaps they'll just talk to each other over the top of my head! Why doesn't Aunt Adelaide have more babies?"

"If Sir John could see you now, Vicky," replied Lehzen firmly, "he'd be as pleased as Punch. He looks like Mr Punch, come to think of it, with that great big sticking-out chin. If you go on crying, you'll melt into a puddle and they'll come and clear you up, and there won't be any of you left to be Queen!'

"Why does my mother like him?" cried Victoria. "I can't talk to her any more. Why does she always take his side?"

"Half the time," said Lehzen, "she can't understand him. You know she's got no ear for English. If she knew what he was saying, she wouldn't like him,

I'm sure. But it's hard to tell her."

Victoria sat straight up in bed and banged her fists down on the sheets over and over again. "I HATE THEM BOTH!" she yelled. Then she began to sob from deep down in her stomach, and went on crying until she was nearly sick.

Lehzen didn't like Sir John Conroy either. But if she said so to the Duchess, then the Duchess would tell Sir John and he would order Lehzen to be sent away, and then, where would Victoria be without her? Lehzen knew she must keep quiet.

"Take no notice of him, Vicky!" she said lightly. "Pretend he's a spider in the corner of the ceiling! Or a beetle running along the floor. Or pretend he's not there at all – that you're just imagining him. Then you can imagine him away again whenever you like! One day, you know, he won't be there. As soon as you're Queen, you can put him in the Tower and have his head chopped off!" And she brought Victoria a hanky and a glass of milk.

Next morning, Sir John asked Victoria to lend him her pocket-money for a whole week, and when she wouldn't, he said she was stingy.

"Just like your grandmother Queen Charlotte," he said, "you know, the wife of your dotty old grandfather King George the Third. One sandwich short of a picnic, he was! But I expect they've told you about him."

Victoria stood there calmly, imagining he wasn't there. Then a little smile began at the corner of her mouth. She was thinking about all the things she could do to Sir John Conroy once she was Queen. Like putting him in the Tower and having his head chopped off. Or pulling out all the hairs on his head one by one, and then all the hairs *inside his nose.* Oh, yes. There were possibilities, once you put your mind to it.

Or, thought Victoria, *I might just put creepy-crawlies down the back of his neck, and leave it at that.*

Chapter Thirteen

Sir John Conroy had a daughter who was tall and dark like him, with slanty, slitty eyes. She was the same age as Victoria, and she too was called after Victory. Her name was Victoire. When they were small, she and Victoria had played together.

But as they grew up, Victoria began to feel uncomfortable.

It's as if she's watching me, she thought, *out of the corner of her eye. Waiting for me to drop something, or knock something over. Or fall down. Or cry, or feel ill. Why?*

"You look pale today," Victoire would say, when Victoria was feeling perfectly well. "Wouldn't you like to lie down?" And Victoria would start to feel ill and want to lie down.

Or she would ask Victoria about her grandfather King George the Third. "Is it true that he was one fishfork short of a dinner set?" asked Victoire, and giggled, all slanty and slitty.

"I don't know what you mean," said Victoria, although she could guess.

"Father says he was," said Victoire, and giggled again.

"There's some truth in it," said Lehzen later. "Your poor old grandfather. Not his fault. He wasn't a bad king, as they go. Cared about his people, didn't throw money away, took an interest in what was going on. There have been worse."

They were out trotting in the park one chilly afternoon in March, well wrapped up. Victoria often told Lehzen things like this when they were out riding, and felt better afterwards.

"And as for Miss Victoire Conroy, what else do you expect?" sniffed Lehzen. "She's her father's daughter, isn't she? She doesn't really mean any harm, poor thing. When you catch her staring at you, stare back." And they broke into a canter, to keep warm.

Victoria tried staring back, and felt better. And she drew Victoire watching her, slitty-eyed. Victoire, who hated the drawing, was watching for signs of Victoria being not quite right in the head, like her grandfather. Victoire was doing so, of course, under secret orders from her father.

"If we can prove that the child's batty," Sir John said to himself in his cold little bedroom, "we can lock her up in Windsor Castle! Or the Tower of London!" *And then*, he thought, studying himself in the mirror. *They'll let the Duchess rule England for a bit, while they sort themselves out!* And he smirked in the mirror.

"They'll have to!" agreed his handsome reflection. "Wicked Uncle Ernest can't come near the Throne while Victoria's alive!"

"So he can't!" rejoiced Sir John, beaming happily at his reflection. "He won't be allowed to!

Even if she's locked in the Tower! They'll have to have the Duchess! Yippee! She can hand the cash over to me! I'll give her a bit back, I suppose, and the odd threepence for little Eggface." And he performed a pirouette in front of the mirror, all eyes and teeth.

His reflection pirouetted back.

All Victoria understood was, she must be on her guard every minute of the time.

Chapter Fourteen

When Uncle William and Aunt Adelaide had been on the Throne for a while with no more babies, the Government passed a new law: Victoria would be the next Queen. But if King William should die before she was eighteen, when she could be Queen on her own, then her mother would rule England until her birthday. This new law made Uncle Ernest furious and Sir John very happy.

Hooray! he thought, finishing a cheese sandwich in bed, *Uncle William can't last long – he's too old and red in the face. We'll have the Duchess as Regent soon, being advised by You Know Who.* Then he wiped the last crumbs off his lips and smiled encouragingly at his reflection. It grinned back. His spirits soared. "I don't see what we're waiting for," he said to himself. "Old fool's as good as dead."

And he began to urge the Duchess to be rude to Uncle William and Aunt Adelaide.

"They're as good as dead." said Sir John. "You're Queen of England, give or take a few. Why don't you behave like Her?"

"Dat's qvite right!" agreed the Duchess, and she began to be rude to Uncle William. But he could see what was in her mind, and in Sir John Conroy's mind.

I don't feel like kicking the bucket just yet, thought Uncle William to himself. *I want to be King first, for a bit. After all, I waited until I was sixty-five.*

And Uncle William decided to take his medicines and do his exercises, and eat proper food, though not too much, and to go on being King for as long as possible, in order to annoy the Duchess and Sir John Conroy.

Chapter Fifteen

Soon the Government decided to give the Duchess more money, so that she could give grand parties in Kensington Palace, and dances and concerts; and so that she could dress Victoria, who was now fourteen, in elegant clothes from Paris, with enamel bracelets and sapphire necklaces and earrings to bring out the blue of her eyes. These still bulged a bit, and she still didn't have much chin. Worse, she hadn't grown much, except for her hair. This bothered her most. Lehzen began to study fashion magazines.

"I know!' she said one day. "Let's do your hair in a long plait, and then wind it round and round your head, like a crown. Then you'll look taller, and as queenly as anything! Can't wait to see it!"

And all of a sudden, there was Princess Victoria looking three inches taller and as queenly as anything, just as Lehzen had said.

And when Victoria began to stay up late for the parties and dinners and concerts in her sapphire

earrings and queenly plait, she could feel everyone looking at her and admiring her – except Sir John Conroy, of course.

By now, the Duchess was taking her daughter on journeys all over England in elegant coaches and carriages. They tied bows and pink ribbons and bunches of flowers on to the horses, and the Duchess and Victoria looked lovely, and the people were glad to see them. They spent many nights in castles and stately homes all over England, being polite to the owners. Victoria admired silver and statues and wooden carvings, and birds made out of sparkling precious stones, and embroideries hanging on walls, and pictures of their great-uncle's stepmother's aunts, until she was tired out.

"How lovely" she said,

and, "How interesting!"

and, "Isn't that beautiful?"

over and over again.

The owners of the castles were very pleased. This was good practice for being Queen.

And they went to the Midlands, to watch the poor people digging up coal. *Everything here was black,* wrote

Victoria, who by now was writing down what she did every day in a little book. *The houses were all black, the tiny huts and farms were black, the cows and pigs and horses and geese were black.*

The poor people were black too, covered with coal dust, and very, very hungry and thin. Victoria never forgot what she saw in the Midlands. This, too, was good practice for being Queen.

Chapter Sixteen

Victoria had one useful uncle who behaved well, on the whole. His name was Leopold. He was the Duchess of Kent's brother, and he was very clever. So much so, in fact, that two entirely different countries which didn't have a king said to him:

"Please come and be our King!"

and he had to choose.

The first of these countries was Greece, a beautiful, ancient country on the Mediterranean Sea. It had hot weather, a lovely seaside and wonderful mountains and ancient temples and palaces.

"I wouldn't mind Greece," said Uncle Leopold. "I could sit in the sun and draw pictures of the palaces and temples, and swim in the sea, and eat olives and goat's cheese − when I wasn't working hard at being King, of course."

Victoria looked at her map of the world and found Greece.

"It's hundreds of miles away!" she said. "Please don't go so far away! I should miss you, dear Uncle."

"Oh," said Uncle Leopold "Oh. Oh dear." And he looked sad. "Then," he said "I shall have to choose Belgium."

Belgium is a newish country and it was even newer then, made up out of left-over bits of France and Germany and Holland after the Boney Wars. It was rainy and cold and mostly flat, with no temples or sea or ancient palaces.

All in all, thought Uncle Leopold, *it couldn't be more different from Greece.*

But even so, he chose to be King of Belgium

in order to be near his niece Victoria, and to go on being as useful to her as he could. From time to time, though, he thought longingly of Greece, with its olives and temples and goat's cheese.

Uncle Leopold didn't want another Boney coming along. And he wanted Victoria to be a good queen, not a bad one like the last real Queen of England, Anne, who had been Queen on her own before the first King George.

"Anne wasn't a good queen," said Uncle Leopold one morning, frowning. He was giving Victoria a history lesson in her schoolroom.

"Why?" asked Victoria, writing it down. "What did Anne do wrong?"

"She was weak," answered Uncle Leopold. "She let other people make her mind up for her. A queen should be strong and make up her own mind sometimes, though not always. And she should have a true heart."

"What's that?" asked Victoria, concentrating. This morning was proving hard work.

"If your heart is true," explained Uncle Leopold, slowly and carefully, "you keep asking yourself what you really feel, what you really think about what you are saying and doing. Then you answer yourself honestly, even if you'd rather not. Then you listen to the answer. Then you think about it. And then you tell other people. That can be tricky."

"Do you have to tell them?" asked Victoria, still writing. Her wrist ached and she was starting to get a headache.

"Not always," said Uncle Leopold. "Telling them may be dangerous or a bad idea. You have to decide. And while you're thinking about it, you can't go to sleep."

"It sounds like what I do anyway!" said Victoria, suddenly remembering. "It's what Lehzen says! Only more so." And she put her pen down and rested her aching wrist.

"Then you'll manage," answered Uncle Leopold. "All you need is practice. And you'll get plenty of that."

Chapter Seventeen

Just before Victoria's seventeenth birthday, two of her young German cousins came to stay at the Palace. They arrived with their father, Duke Ferdinand, another brother of Victoria's mother.

The older cousin was training to be the next Duke. He was dark, with a nice smile. He didn't talk much. His younger brother Albert did the talking. Albert was tall, with a very straight nose and the right amount of chin. His eyes and hair were exactly the same colour as Victoria's.

"We could be twins," she said.

"In a way," said Albert, smiling, "we are. I was born exactly one month after you, to the day. And our mothers were looked after by the same doctor, who was a woman!"

"Really?" said Victoria.

"The first woman doctor in Germany," said Albert. "She came to England with your mother, and then rushed back to Germany after you were born,

in time for me. So we were brought into the world by the same person!"

"Only," said Victoria, trying to stand on tiptoe, "you're twice as tall as I am."

"Perhaps you haven't finished growing yet," suggested Albert kindly. "You'll shoot right up, I'm sure."

They had brought Victoria a big parrot as a present. She already had a sort of parrot, small and grey. This new one was scarlet and yellow and brown and blue and purple and green – and tame, too! She could watch it and talk to it for hours. Both the brothers liked animals and birds as much as she did.

"That's because of our tutor," said Albert "He's taught me to make bird noises. I can whistle like a nightingale and get another one to answer me. I like dogs, too, and they like me."

When Dash set eyes on Cousin Albert, he began to bark and jump about, wanting to be friends. Then he stood still patiently while Albert tied bows of red ribbon round his ears.

"But Dash never stands still!" said Victoria, amazed. "Not even for me! Except when I bath him. He loves that better than anything."

"Do you bath him yourself?" asked Albert, surprised.

"Every night," said Victoria. "No matter what. Lehzen holds him and I wash him. We all get wet. Then he has his biscuit."

"May I watch?" asked Albert.

"You can help!" said Victoria firmly, and that evening Albert got soaked to the skin.

Albert enjoyed drawing, too, and music. He liked playing the piano while Victoria sang. Nobody listened, so it didn't matter if they made mistakes.

Isn't it amazing, thought Victoria, *to have a friend of my own age who likes what I like! I've never had that before, never ever.*

But in the evenings Albert was a bit odd.

He couldn't keep his eyes open after nine o'clock at night, even for dinner.

"Sorry," he would say, yawning into his soup, "I need lots of sleep. I always have done." His head would fall into the soup with a jerk, and a waiter would have to come and mop him up.

At Victoria's seventeenth birthday party, Albert danced with her twice, beautifully. Then he turned the colour of a potato, and yawned.

"Sorry, Victoria," he said, "I must go to bed."

Victoria danced until four in the morning, fresh as a daisy. *Poor Albert,* she thought, looking round the gaily decorated ballroom, with its twinkling cut-glass chandeliers. He hadn't enjoyed looking at them, or listening to the thrilling brass band of the Grenadier Guards.

What a shame, thought Victoria. *We've had such fun in the daytimes.* For a moment she felt sad. Still, perhaps Cousin Albert would return to England one day, when he'd caught up with his sleep, and tie more red ribbon round Dash's ears, and play more music with her.

Chapter Eighteen

Uncle William developed asthma, a painful disease which makes it hard to breathe.

Sir John Conroy was very pleased.

"Princess," he said to Victoria, "When you become Queen of England, you're going to need a Private Secretary."

"What's that?" asked Victoria. She was lying in bed ill. She had a headache and a fever. Marie Taglioni lay in one arm. With her other hand, Victoria could just reach Dash's paw. He was stretched on the carpet, as near as he could get to her head.

"A very important person," said Sir John, "highly paid, who decides things for the Queen. Why not give the job to me?"

"No," said Victoria, thinking of weak Queen Anne. "No, I don't think so."

"I'd be rather good at it," said Sir John, leaning against the mantelpiece and crossing his legs.

"Being Queen is all about money, though people pretend it isn't. You need someone who knows about money. You don't. You're a girl. You need someone who can collect it for you. Me."

"I have such a headache." said Victoria, holding Marie Taglioni tight.

Sir John Conroy took no notice. He uncrossed his legs, came and sat on the end of her bed, and crossed them again. Dash growled.

"Once you're Queen," said Sir John, shifting his feet, "they give you a large purse. It's called a Privy Purse, and it's yours. You're supposed to keep it full. From time to time people have to put money into it. But they won't, if you don't make them. People are awful. You need somebody to write letters telling them to pay up, and telling them what'll happen to them if they don't — and to their mothers and fathers and their aunties in the country. Then they pay up, as a rule.

79

Do you follow me so far?"

"I feel sick," said Victoria.

"Once you've got their money," continued Sir John, one eye on Dash, "you won't know how to spend it. You haven't had any practice. I can help you," he said kindly. "I can spend your money and you can watch. You'll soon get the hang of it. It's boring, of course. You may not feel like watching all the time. But that's all right. I don't mind doing it on my own for a bit, without you, so you can get on with being a girl."

"I wish you'd go away." said Victoria. And Marie Taglioni said, "Go away," but very quietly. Dash barked.

"Nasty brute." said Sir John. "Once you've made me your Private Secretary, I'll go away. Now," he said, "sit up. Take this pen. Write your name at the bottom of this important piece of paper – neatly, mind."

"I won't," said Victoria. "I'm not going to write my name at the bottom of anything."

She threw the pen into a corner of the room and pulled the sheet over her head. Her head ached and her back ached and she felt sick. But she knew she must say no to all Sir John Conroy's bad ideas.

"Well, then," he said, standing over her bed, "you'll have to be punished. You're not Queen yet. You still have to do what I tell you."

"No, I don't," said Victoria through the sheet, hugging Marie Taglioni. "Go away!"

Lehzen, too, said, "Go away, Sir John." She had been standing there quietly, listening.

"AAARRGH," growled Dash, close to Sir John's feet. Sir John leapt up, then perched on Victoria's bedside table.

"In that case," he threatened, up in the air, "I shall tell your mother to lock you in a cupboard until you change your mind! You know she always does what I say!"

"Perhaps she won't, this time!" yelled Victoria through the sheet, although she wasn't sure. "Go away!"

And in the end he went.

Victoria was right: the Duchess refused to lock her daughter in a cupboard. She loved her, deep down. It was just that Sir John Conroy kept telling her that he knew best, and that he was her only friend, and she believed him.

Next day, Victoria was even iller. "Please," she begged, "Would you send for the doctor?"

"Rubbish!" said Sir John. "You're making it up. You're trying to attract attention. Get out of bed, and don't be silly."

But Victoria really was ill – so ill that her hair began to fall out. Lehzen became frightened that she might die.

"The doctor's away for a few days," said Sir John. "Today's Wednesday. He'll be back on Friday. Here's a bottle of vegetable syrup. He left it for Victoria, in case she keeps on making a fuss."

"Vegetable syrup is for tummy upsets!" retorted Lehzen. "It's for people who eat and drink too much, like Victoria's Uncle George. Victoria hasn't eaten anything for days. She's boiling hot. She's got a headache and backache and her hair is falling out."

"No, it isn't," said Sir John Conroy, though he could see it was.

"Yes, it is, you appalling man," said Lehzen. "You can see it is."

"Look," said Sir John. "As I said, the doctor can't come till Friday. Can't it wait a couple of days? If I get another doctor in, the whole country will know. What will they say?"

"I don't care," said Lehzen, "and neither should you. What I care about is Princess Victoria's health. She might die — but I won't let her. Send for another doctor, you walking apology for a human being, and get cracking."

"I'll think about it," said Sir John, sulkily, and he went away and thought about it. He wanted Victoria to stay ill and weak and unfit to be Queen, but he didn't want her to die. If she did, then Uncle Ernest would become King, the Duchess would never be Princess Regent and Sir John wouldn't get anywhere near the Privy Purse.

So he sent for another doctor, who gave Victoria proper medicine and made her breathe lots of fresh air. Soon she started to feel better. Her back and her head stopped hurting, and she stopped feeling hot all over. She began to eat boring things like spinach soup and dry toast and baked parsnips, and after a while she was well again.

Her almond hair grew again, too, longer and shinier than ever.

Chapter Nineteen

The Duchess of Kent and Uncle William annoyed each other more and more.

Please can Victoria come to tea, wrote Aunt Adelaide to the Duchess, in beautiful handwriting. *We've got chocolate sponge cake and iced biscuits and strawberry jelly and cream.*

Sorry, the Duchess wrote back, in beautiful handwriting. *No.*

Why not? wrote Aunt Adelaide, (because the phone hadn't been invented yet).

Because I don't feel like letting her, wrote back the Duchess. *So there.*

Some more of the Duchess's German relations came to London, and wanted to meet the King and Queen and have tea at St James's Palace.

Sorry, wrote Uncle William, in beautiful handwriting, *they're not Royal Blood. I don't have to invite them. I've checked up. Besides, I don't feel like it.*

Then Victoria and the Duchess went on holiday again, all over the country.

"Soldiers! Boom de guns!" ordered the Duchess of Kent with sparkling eyes, everywhere they went. "Sailors! Pull up de huge flak of Englant! You see here your new younk Qveen!" And the soldiers and sailors fired guns and hauled up the national flag, as if Victoria were already Queen.

This annoyed Uncle William still more.

Then Victoria's mother did something even worse. The ground floor of Kensington Palace, where they lived, was gloomy and dark. The Duchess decided to move them both on to the floor above, with bright, cheerful rooms and a wonderful view over the whole park. The King owned the palace, so she should have asked him first, but didn't. When he found out, just before breakfast, his face went blotchy and reddish-mauve. He started to wheeze.

"Finish your grouse, dear," said Queen Adelaide over the polished table. "And your kidneys and your fish pie. Breathe deeply. Try not to get cross. You know it brings on your asthma."

"I don't care two hoots if it does," wheezed Uncle William. He sent his gold-rimmed breakfast plate sliding down the long table. "I might not have minded so much," he went on, "if only that woman had asked me first. But she didn't. And I do mind."

Uncle William ground his teeth noisily. His face went almost black.

"I'm sick to death of the Duchess of Kent," he said. "I'm going to give her hell. In front of as many people as possible…"

Chapter Twenty

It was Uncle William's birthday. He was having a grand celebration in the sparkly gilt drawing-room at Windsor Castle. Over a hundred guests stood uncomfortably about in their best clothes and shoes, chit-chatting. The ladies wore tall feathers standing straight up on top of their heads, in honour of the King.

The Duchess of Kent arrived late, dressed in gold. Her feathers were twice the height of anyone else's. As she and Victoria entered the drawing-room, Uncle William got up slowly, clutching the arms of his chair. First he kissed Victoria, to show he wasn't angry with her. Then he turned to the Duchess of Kent. The sight of her particularly tall feathers made him crosser than ever, which brought on his asthma.

"Madam," he wheezed, "You've been insulting me for years. This is the final straw."

The hundred guests forgot their discomfort. They stopped chatting with each other and watched

the King, who glared ferociously at the startled Duchess.

"How dare you take over those nice rooms without asking me first?" exploded Uncle William. "They're my rooms. They're part of the Privy Purse. You make me sick."

He wheezed louder, his eyes popping dangerously out of his head.

The Duchess of Kent burned red.

Aunt Adelaide turned pale.

Victoria went bright pink.

"So, just to annoy you," continued the king, "I'm going to make jolly sure I stay alive until after Victoria's eighteenth birthday, which isn't long now. Then she can be Queen all by herself. I think she'll be good. I think you'd be a rotten Princess Regent and so would your slimy friend Sir John Conroy, if you see what I mean."

The King was beginning to enjoy himself. The hundred guests were enjoying it too. The Duchess of Kent burst into tears. So did Aunt Adelaide and so did Victoria. None of them said a word. The king breathed more deeply. His voice grew stronger.

"And while I'm about it," he went on, "will you please let Victoria come to tea with Aunt Adelaide and me sometimes? We really like her, not having any princesses of our own. We want to be friends. So stop throwing your weight about. And why can't you wear medium-sized feathers on your head, like other people? You make me sick, as I've said. There, now." he said, sitting down again and feeling better than he had for months.

The hundred guests each felt as if they had been given a Christmas present — a piece of gossip to pass on to their friends and relations, together with a fine excuse for boasting about where they'd been.

The Duchess of Kent felt terrible for three days. Then she got over it.

Chapter Twenty-One

One month later came Victoria's own birthday, an important one. She was eighteen.

The Duchess of Kent gave her diamond earrings and a ruby necklace, which Victoria wore to her big party. Lehzen gave her an enamel bracelet, a pin cushion and an embroidered Chinese shawl. Victoire Conroy gave her a handkerchief case embroidered with silver.

Sir John Conroy gave her a picture of himself.

One of Victoria's nicest presents came from Dash (who must have asked Lehzen what she thought Victoria might like). It was a little ivory basket filled with chocolates and barley sugar twirls. Victoria shared the chocolates and barley sugar with Lehzen, and kept her new earrings in the ivory basket.

But next morning when she tried to thank Dash, he growled and went silent. All day he lay curled in his basket. He wouldn't come out for breakfast, tea or dinner. That evening, while running his bath, Victoria suddenly remembered.

"Dearest Dash," she said, "Last night I forgot to bath you! Please forgive me! It was my birthday party, after all, and I was excited about being eighteen."

The dog looked at her coldly out of one eye.

"I look forward to my evening bath, you know," he said. "There's not much in a palace for a dog to be getting on with."

"I really am sorry," said Victoria. "I won't do it again, I promise. Please forgive me. I've been worrying about you all day."

Slowly Dash uncurled, climbed out of his basket and came towards her.

"Don't forget me again, ever," he said. "Mind you don't." And he lay down on the floor in front of her. "Now, rub my tummy."

"I *am* sorry," she said, rubbing. "Dearest Dashy."

"Well, that's all right, then!" said Dash. After that, he had an extra biscuit and a good scratch.

"Never again," said Victoria. "No matter what."

Chapter Twenty-Two

One morning early in June, the Duchess of Kent woke Victoria. She did so gently, by stroking her ear. Then she said urgently, "Get up, Vicky! De Archbishop of Canterbury vants to see you! In ze sittink room. Widout me. Widout Lehzen. Alone!"

Victoria put on her dressing-gown and shawl, and went into her small, red-patterned sitting-room. And there was the Archbishop of Canterbury, who was very old, on his knees on the carpet.

"Princess Victoria," he said, "You know that your poor Uncle King William the Fourth has been ill for a long time. Well, I'm sorry to say he's passed away. At twelve minutes past two this morning, to be precise. And so," said the Archbishop, "you are now Queen of England."

He kissed Victoria's hand, got up creakily from his knees, brushed the carpet fluff off his breeches and left the room – bumping into the Duchess of Kent, who had been listening outside the door.

"Darlink Vicky! At last!" beamed the Duchess, rushing in. "You're Qveen! I must go and tell tear Sir John! Von't he be thrilled!" She gave Victoria a quick kiss and swept off to tell the news to him.

Victoria went slowly back to the bedroom she had shared all her life with her mother. And there was Lehzen, who silently helped Victoria on with her clothes, then hugged her for about three minutes.

Dash came leaping in from his basket outside, and licked Victoria's face.

"I'm Queen, Dash!" said Victoria.

"I always thought you were, anyway," barked Dash. "Where's breakfast?"

And Victoria and Lehzen and Dash went to the kitchen and ate bacon and eggs and sausage and mushrooms and tomatoes and toast and honey and three cups of tea each.

Victoria gave Dash her bacon rind and half a sausage. She ate silently, thinking: *There's a lot I don't know. But I do know how to stand up to Sir John Conroy. And I think I know how to keep a true heart. I'm going to get down to being Queen. I'm going to give Being Her all I've got.* Then she thought,

Poor Aunt Adelaide. She'll miss Uncle William.

After breakfast, Victoria wrote a letter to Windsor Castle:

> *Dear Aunt Adelaide,*
>
> *I'm really sorry about Uncle William. Please stay in Windsor Castle as long as you like, even though I'm supposed to live there now, instead.*
>
> *Lots of love,*
> *Victoria (Queen)*
>
> *P.S. Let's have tea soon.*

Then she wrote to Belgium.

> *Dear Uncle Leopold,*
>
> *Poor Uncle William has died, so I'm Queen.*
>
> *Lots of love,*
> *Victoria (Queen)*
>
> *P.S. Thanks for being so useful.*

And then she wrote to Germany:

Dearest Feodora,

I'm Queen!!!

Masses of love,
Vicky (Queen)

P.S. What fun!!!

Then Victoria and Dash went to the stables, to say good morning to Rosa, to give her a sugar lump and to pat her.

"And now," said Victoria, "We'd better go back to the palace and see the dolls. I haven't seen them for a while now. Let's start with Marie Taglioni."

So they went and found Marie Taglioni, who was lying in a box on her own.

"You're a queen's doll now," said Victoria. "You must have

a new dress. Pink and silver and sea-green, with lace. You'll look lovely." And Marie Taglioni seemed to smile.

"I still love you," said Victoria. "I'm busier now, that's all."

"You'd better not treat me like you treat her," barked Dash, "Ever. No matter how busy you are."

Chapter Twenty-Three

That morning, Victoria saw her Prime Minister alone.

"Do you like dogs?" she asked him, among other things.

"Very much indeed, ma'am," said the Prime Minister. She could see that they were going to be friends.

At eleven o'clock that morning, Victoria held her first Council Meeting with her Ministers. They all kissed her hand and said she was wonderful and how glad they were she was Queen. Anyone would enjoy all that, and she did.

And now, she thought, *I need a room of my own. You can't have a queen who still shares a room with her mother. Besides, I don't want to hear Sir John Conroy's name ever again.*

So she asked for a bedroom of her own, and got it. The Duchess was hurt, and it took her a long time to understand, but she did in the end.

Sir John made a great fuss and asked for a lot of money, but in the end he vanished, more or less, as Lehzen had said. Victoria had put up with him for years, and now she didn't have to any more. Later, she found out that he had been stealing money from her mother. The Duchess was deeply shocked. In the end she was grateful to Victoria for getting rid of him.

Chapter Twenty-Four

One year later, Victoria went to Westminster Abbey to be crowned Queen. She had to wake up at four o'clock in the morning. They dressed her in red velvet, white satin and lace with gold threads, and a gold coronet on her head sparkling with diamonds. The huge Abbey was hung with red and gold, with Chinese carpets on the floor. There were Dukes and Duchesses and Earls and Marquises and Ministers covered in jewels from head to foot. And there were trumpets and drums and a choir singing, and guns going off.

Bishops in long, curly, grey wigs were everywhere, and didn't seem to know what they were supposed to be doing – not even the old Archbishop of Canterbury.

But at last he picked up the Crown, covered with sapphires and rubies, and put it on Victoria's head as she sat on the Throne, pressing it down much too tight, while the choir sang like angels. Then the Dukes and Duchesses and Earls and Marquises took their own

little coronets, which they had been holding in their hands, and put them on their own heads, sparkling and shining.

They look like the stars in the Milky War, thought Victoria, *and the singing's beautiful. And it's all for me. If it weren't for my finger and my head, I would think I'd died and gone to heaven.*

Victoria's finger was hurting, because the Archbishop had tried to cram a tiny ring on to one of her bigger fingers.

"I'm sure that's the wrong finger," she said politely. "I think it's meant for my little finger."

"No it isn't," said the Archbishop, pushing it on even tighter.

"Ow!" said Victoria. But she smiled and looked queenly, even though her finger was hurting her. Lehzen looked so proud, sitting in a royal box just above the Throne. She smiled at Victoria, and Victoria smiled back.

Then Victoria had to walk all the way back down the long Abbey, wearing the heavy Crown and a heavier gold train, with the Royal Ball in one hand and the Royal Pole in the other. They were gold, but they felt more like lead.

I've had enough, thought Victoria, staggering to the door. *I want to sit down and take all this off, and have dinner and a talk with my Prime Minister. He looks tired, too.*

But there was one more thing she must do first. A Queen of England must keep a true heart. And there was something Victoria had promised never to forget again, no matter what.

Bath Dash.

As the Royal Carriage reached the palace courtyard, there he was, waiting on the steps, waving

his feathery tail. What difference did her being crowned make to him? And where had she been all day?

Victoria's head ached, and her back ached, and her finger hurt like anything.

"But I'm not letting Dash down again," she said to herself. "No. Not for the world."

The coach rolled into the courtyard and stopped. Victoria took off her crown, nearly dropping it, and gave it to her Prime Minister to hold. Then she gathered up her skirt and leapt out of the carriage door, across the courtyard and up the palace steps, to reward the most loving subject in her whole Queendom – to give Dash his biscuit and his royal bath.

Important dates in
H.R.H. Princess Victoria's early life

1819 Princess Victoria is born to Edward Duke of Kent and his German wife Victoire.

1820 Victoria's father dies.

1828 Feodora, daughter of Victoire, Princess of Leiningen (later Duchess of Kent) and Prince Charles of Leiningen marries Prince Ernest of Hohenlohe Langenburg and goes to live in Germany.

1830 King George the Fourth dies and Victoria's Uncle William becomes King William III.

1832 Victoria visits the Midlands.

1835 Victoria is extremely ill.

1836 Victoria's German cousins Prince Ernest the Elder and Prince Albert come to stay. King William III's 72nd birthday.

1837 Victoria's 18th birthday. Uncle William dies and Victoria becomes Queen.

Kings and Queens of England since 1066

House of Normandy
WILLIAM I 1066–1087
WILLIAM II 1087–1100
HENRY I 1100–1135
STEPHEN 1135–1154
EMPRESS MATILDA (QUEEN MAUD) 1141

House of Plantagenet
HENRY II 1154–1189
RICHARD I 1189–1199
JOHN 1199–1216
HENRY III 1216–1272
EDWARD I 1272–1307
EDWARD II 1307–1327
EDWARD III 1327–1377
RICHARD II 1377–1399

House of Lancaster
HENRY IV 1399–1413
HENRY V 1413–1422
HENRY VI 1422–1461

House of York
EDWARD IV 1461–1483
EDWARD V 1483
RICHARD III 1483–1485

House of Tudor
HENRY VII 1485–1509
HENRY VIII 1509–1547
EDWARD VI 1547–1553
JANE GREY 1553
MARY I 1553–1558
ELIZABETH I 1558–1603

House of Stuart
JAMES I 1603–1625
CHARLES I 1625–1649

Commonwealth
OLIVER CROMWELL 1653–1658
RICHARD CROMWELL 1658–1659

House of Stuart (restored)
Charles II 1660–1685
James II 1685–1688
William III 1689–1702
Mary II 1689–1694
Anne 1702–1714

House of Hanover
George I 1714–1727
George II 1727–1760
George III 1760–1820
George IV 1820–1830
William IV 1830–1837
Victoria 1837–1901

House of Saxe-Coburg-Gotha
Edward VII 1901–1910

House of Windsor
George V 1910–1936
Edward VIII 1936–1936
George VI 1936–1952
Elizabeth II 1952 – reigning

KARIN FERNALD

is an actor who has played roles ranging from
Sally Bowles in *Cabaret* to the Dormouse in
Alice in Wonderland. She is known for her lectures
and solo shows on Hans Christian Andersen,
Fanny Burney, Florence Nightingale and other
18th and 19th-century writers and artists, whom
she brings to vivid life through diaries and letters.
She has taken her shows round the world. Karin was
attracted to Queen Victoria by her paintings and
drawings, and by the young queen's hilarious
account of her coronation.